# Nessie the Mannerless Monster

# Nessie the Mannerless Monster

## Ted Hughes

*illustrated by Gerald Rose*

*faber and faber*

LONDON · BOSTON

First published in 1964
by Faber and Faber Limited
3 Queen Square London WC1N 3AU
This paperback edition first published in 1992

Photoset by Parker Typesetting Service, Leicester
Printed in England by Clays Ltd, St Ives plc

Ted Hughes is hereby identified as author of this work and Gerald
Rose as illustrator in accordance with Section 77 of the Copyright,
Designs and Patents Act 1988

A CIP record for this book is available from the British Library

ISBN 0-571-16213-4

# Nessie the Mannerless Monster

In Scotland is a Loch.
At the bottom of this Loch, in the
    pitch black,
A monster lives, called Nessie. It is just
    her luck.
She is about the size of a truck,
But shaped like an old sock,
With a long worm of a neck.
She is beginning to feel sick.

She is sick with sorrow. 'Nobody thinks
   I exist.
They all say my time has passed.
They say I am a fairy beast.
I do not want to boast,
But I will make myself known or bust.'
So Nessie rises in a great burst
Of spray, she smashes the water to mist,
She scuds around doing her worst.

But people just keep on driving past.
They say: 'No, No! Such things do not
    exist.'
Soon she grows tired and has to lie there,
    having a rest.

Then in a rage, she outs on to the road.
She says: 'I don't want to be rude,
But after all, I have my pride.'
She says: 'I am going to make a raid
On Edinburgh.' Then all the tourists
   cried
'What's that? What's that? Oh, Oh, let me
   hide!'
And they crashed their cars into the
   roadside.
They covered their eyes hoping the sight
   would fade.
But Nessie walked straight on, she paid no
   heed.

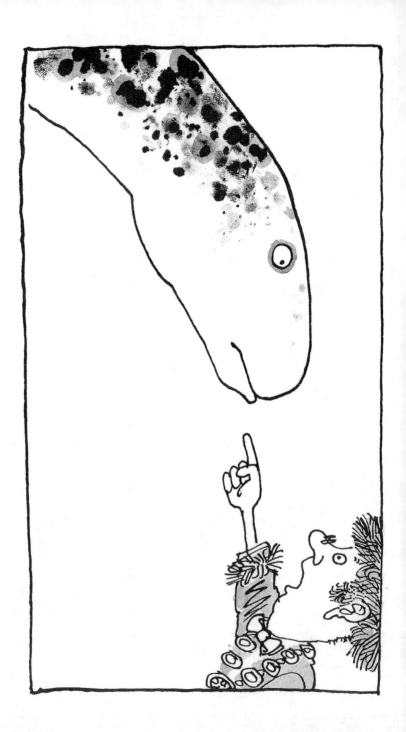

The Mayor of Edinburgh nearly had a fit
When he saw Nessie. 'Look at it! Look at
    it!'
He cried, and fainted right there on the
    spot.

But the police said, 'Whose is that huge
    cat?
It is blocking our traffic more than a bit.
Divert it south to London.' So that was
    that.
Nessie had not opened her mouth and she
    was out,
Tramping south towards London alone
    and on foot.

As she was tramping down through
  Northumberland
Up out of a ditch pops this fox-hound.
'Look!' he howls, 'A fox as long as a brass
  band!'
The other hounds come running up and
  all stare stunned.
Then Wow-wow-wow! they chase Nessie
  over the ploughed land,
And into a wood and out at the far end,
Then into a meadow and round with the
  cows and round.

'I'm no fox,' cries Nessie, but they can't
    understand.
She dives into and just fills up a
    duckpond.
The huntsmen gallop up. When they see
    Nessie making a stand
They turn away their horses and tuck their
    hounds under
Their arms and creep off home quaking
    with fear and no wonder,
Seeing Nessie there in the duckpond like
    a coal-black forty-foot gander.

She marches south into Yorkshire, the
   greatest shire.
'Now,' she says, 'I've heard there are
   honest folk here
Who will all cry "Nessie!" the minute I
   appear.'
But what does she find? The streets are all
   empty and bare.
Everybody sits indoors in front of the TV
   with a dead stare.

There is nothing in the streets but cats,
  dogs and the odd parked car.
She peers in at the windows and whistles
  but nobody can hear
For the TV and its laughter and uproar
  and gunfire.
There is no other sign of life in all
  Yorkshire anywhere,
Till she meets a little boy and he shouts:
  'Hey, you. Get out of here.'

Next, travelling through the woods to
    avoid the cars
She meets Sir Mimms Culdimple
    Bagforkhumberly-parse.
'You'll stay to dine,' offers that gent, with
    a laugh, 'of course?'
And he rips off an utterly dumbfounding
    curse
That kills a big orange horsefly on the ear
    of a nearby horse.

Nessie devours partridges, pheasants,
   pigs' heads, pike and parts of hares.
She drinks whisky and wine until it pours
   out of her ears.

Then she snaps up the servants, the cook
 too in spite of his roars.
She swallows a settee for wadding, the
 whole item disappears,
And finishes off her host in one gulp, and
 says: 'That was a solid first course.'
And falls down on the carpet and without
 apology snores –
All of which proves she was completely
 without manners and a perfect monster.

Next, she came up with ten thousand
   people and then some.
They all marched packed together, with
   here and there a drum.
They carry banners with the words: 'Ban
   The Bomb.'
They are laughing and singing and Nessie
   thinks: 'Is this a party? Can I come?'
'Be our mascot,' they cry, 'O peaceful
   beast, beautiful and dumb.'
So Nessie marches along at the head of
   them.

She has no idea what it is all about
But all these people follow her with song
    and dance and shout.
'They are taking me to the Queen,' thinks
    Nessie,
'And the Duke of Edinburgh will say,
    "There's a Bonnie Lassie!"
Then I shall be all right, I shall have class,
And everybody will say, "Oh everybody
    knows Nessie, she's a grand lass."
And all these good people are bringing
    this to pass.'

But when they got to the heart of London
and Trafalgar Square
Somehow everybody disappeared into
thin air
Leaving hundreds of policemen yawning
there.
Whenever she asked a policeman the way
to the Queen, he politely directed her to
the zoo.
And so she followed the policeman's
finger, which is what people in London
do.

When Nessie walked through the zoo
 fence
The gorilla burst his bars and fled into the
 far distance.

The keepers jumped clean out of their
    clothes at the first glance
And hid behind the tigers which stood in a
    dumb trance.

The wolves fell into a dead faint at once.
The elephants gave up all thoughts of
    defence.

The eagles went rigid and cried: 'We are
   only weathervanes.'
The snakes murmured: 'Take no notice of
   us, we are only vines.'

The tortoises pulled in their heads and legs and whispered: 'We are stones.'

The lions lay still with eyes closed and
   tried to look like sand-dunes.
And Nessie wandered around saying: 'Are
   all these creatures Queens?'

Till up came the small mammal-house
    keeper, braver than the rest.
'We have no place,' he said, 'for your sort
    of beast.
Go to Kensington Museum, that would be
    best.
They have all your cousins there, prettily
    encased.
You can meet them all and have a real
    feast.'

'Thank you, thank you!' cried Nessie, 'I
    will do just as you suggest.
I was beginning to feel weary and
    depressed.
I never knew I had cousins. When they see
    me won't they be surprised.'

In Kensington Museum all the curators
    stared.
They stared at Nessie, they had never
    seen anything so weird.

'Where are these cousins of mine of
    whom I have heard?'
Asked Nessie, but everybody went on
    staring, nobody said a word.
'Where are they?' cried Nessie, 'They'll
    tell you I do truly exist,
And that I am not a fairy-beast and not a
    dream-beast.'

Then up spoke a world-famous scientist:
'Impostor! You are impossible! If you
    were extinct and no more
Indeed I would say you were a Plesiosaur.
We have plenty of the bones of that beast
    which in its day was not at all rare.
But all Plesiosaurs, say our books, have
    been dead a million year.
Yet you are alive. Look at you. So who
    knows what you are?
Go away and don't bother us here.'
Then they all hurried to their jobs and left
    Nessie alone in despair.

Nessie wandered sadly along High Street.
'Get a move on,' snarled all the taxi-
   drivers, leaning out.
A huge lorry bumped her backside with
   hoot after hoot.
Tourists gasped: 'Look, quick, another
   famous London sight.'
Londoners thought she was an advert, for
   a circus coming that night.
Policemen roared: 'Drive on the left, idiot,
   not the right.'
What with all the noise and crowds Nessie
   was in a great fright.

But all at once a voice from the crowd
  roared 'Ness!'
Her eyes popped when she heard her
  name, joy made her nearly delirious.

It was a wretched Scots writer of verses,
   Willis by name, and he was penniless,
But he knew a monster when he saw one,
   Oh yes.
'Nessie!' he cried, and he gave her flipper
   a great kiss.
She told him her woes and he cried: 'Alas!
   Alas! Alas!

We shall go without hesitation to the
   palace.
Let me ride and you run.' And so in no
   time they were off at a great pace.

When they galloped up to Buckingham
  Palace, guards barred the way.
'Dogs on a leash,' they ordered, and, 'No
  visitors today.'
So Willis cried: 'The Queen's greatest
  subject has something to say –
Nessie here is the Queen's greatest
  subject, I will have you know.'
But the guards just bristled their
  moustaches, and it was no go.

Whereupon Nessie simply ran over the
   guards and left them looking for their
   hats:
But then the Palace Army, which always
   waits,
The Palace Army which protects the
   Queen from all dangers and frights,

Did not stand staring like dumb mountain
   goats.
They barked commands, scampered to
   their posts, manned their guns, gloated
   through the gunsights,
And Nessie and Willis were at any
   moment about to be blown to bits.

'Stop, stop!' shouted Willis, 'Let's have a peace-talk.'

Then out on to her balcony the Queen came for a look,

Her crown on her head, her stoatskins over her arm, to see this freak.

At the sight of Nessie she uttered a strange croak,

But then, like a true Queen, most politely she spoke:

Saying: 'What do you want, for heaven's sake?'

Then Willis up and gave his speech on
    Nessie's behalf.
In no time at all he told how her times
    were so tough,
In no time at all he told the causes of her
    grief,
Living up there in Scotland, monstrous
    beyond belief.

And the Queen was touched with concern
    for this gigantic national waif.
Then the Duke made a joke, and the
    Queen gave a laugh:
'You shall be Vice-Regent of Scotland,
    Wales and Northern Ireland,' she said,
    'For the rest of your life.'

And so it comes about that Nessie reigns
    in Loch Ness.
On Sundays all along the shores the
    people press,
The bands of the Coldstream Guards and
    Scottish Light Infantry play *en masse*.

Nessie cruises up and down with a
    coronet on her head.
She is delighted, she never had it so good.
And Willis is a Civil Servant, he sees that
    she's well fed,
And he's delighted too, he gets so well
    paid.

And what finer life can there be than
  living on the shores of a marvellous lake
With a pet monster, and doing as you like.
The scientists come in tribes, for a look.
Nessie invents stories about her ancestors
  and they write them all down in their
  book.
And whenever the Queen visits Scotland,
  she visits this Loch,
Then she and Nessie sit sipping tea and
  have a really good talk.